To Tobias
Thomas Taylor

For my great-aunt Eliza Louisa Walton,
forever a child, and for my cousin Jane
Jill Barton

First hardback edition published in Great Britain in 2010 by Boxer Books Limited.
First paperback edition published in Great Britain in 2011 by Boxer Books Limited.

www.boxerbooks.com

The illustrations were prepared using watercolour paints, pencil and graphite stick.
The text is set in Adobe Caslon.

ISBN 978-1-907967-16-0

1 3 5 7 9 10 8 6 4 2

Printed in China

All of our papers are sourced from managed forests and renewable resources.

Little Mouse and the Big Cupcake

Written by Thomas Taylor

Illustrated by Jill Barton

Boxer Books

Little Mouse was scurrying along when he found something.
A chocolate-chip, raspberry-cream cupcake!

"Wow!" cried Little Mouse.

"That looks yummy!
But it's so BIG! How can I get it home?"

Just at that moment, Bird flew down.

So Little Mouse asked if she could help.

"That's much too big for me
to carry!" said Bird.

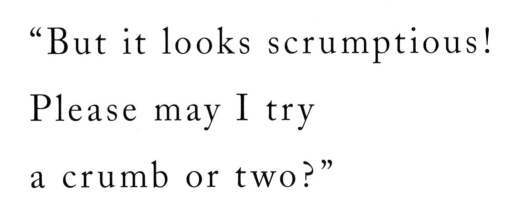

"But it looks scrumptious!
Please may I try
a crumb or two?"

Little Mouse said yes,
and Bird pecked off
a BIG bit.

PIK

PIK

PIK

PIK!

Then along came Frog,
and Little Mouse asked
if he would help.

"I can't lift that!" said Frog.

"It's far too big.

But please may I have a little taste?"

"Of course," said Little Mouse.

Frog took a LARGE bite.

YUM YUM!

Just then, Mole popped his head
out of a hole, so Little Mouse
asked if *he* could help.

"Oh, that's far too big to squeeze
down my tunnel," said Mole.
"But, ooh, please may I have a nibble?"

Little Mouse said okay, and Mole opened his mouth WIDE.

SCRUNCH!

It wasn't long
before other animals
came along.

There was Snail and Possum
and even Chipmunk, and although
none of them could lift the cupcake,
they all asked to try some.

And Little Mouse – being a very kind little mouse – said yes to everyone.

SLURP!
YUM
YUM!

CHOMP CHOMP CHOMP!

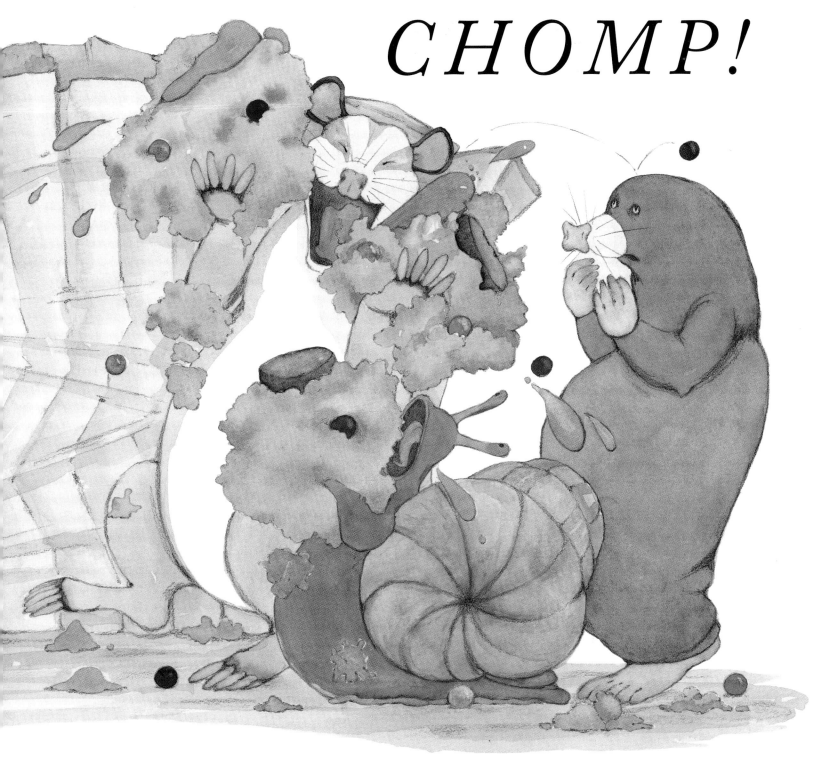

Little Mouse felt sad.
He still didn't know how
he was going to get his
cupcake home.

Then he looked again and noticed
that the cake was smaller now.
MUCH smaller.

In fact, it was exactly mouse size!
"You can carry it now,"
said all of Little Mouse's new friends.

"You're right," cried Little Mouse with
a smile. "It's just the right size to carry ...

in my TUMMY!"

YUMMY!

Other Boxer Books paperbacks

On Our Way Home • Sebastien Braun

Join Daddy Bear and Baby Bear on their journey home, and share their experiences along the way. This heart-warming celebration of the relationship between parent and child is the perfect bedtime read.

ISBN 978-1-906250-80-5

Clip-Clop • Nicola Smee

When Cat, Dog, Pig and Duck climb aboard Mr Horse for a ride, they want to go faster and faster... But will "faster" lead to disaster? A delightful rhythmical text with charming illustrations which will enthral every child.

ISBN 978-1-905417-04-9

Toot Toot Beep Beep • Emma Garcia

Toot Toot Beep Beep is packed with busy busy, noisy noisy vehicles. Little ones will love joining in as colourful cars zoom across the page, each making their own special noise. Perfect for reading aloud!

ISBN 978-1-906250-51-5

Duck & Goose • Tad Hills

Duck and Goose find an egg. "Who does it belong to?" they ask. Duck says it is his because he saw it first. Goose says it is his because he touched it first. Little by little they agree that the most important thing is to look after the egg and decide to share it. But their parenting skills come to an abrupt end when a little bird tells them that their egg is really a ball. Parents everywhere will recognise this tale of one-upmanship which firmly establishes the positive aspects of learning to share.

ISBN 978-1-905417-26-1

www.boxerbooks.com